Debbie's
birthday party

GILBERT DELAHAYE - MARCEL MARLIER

ap
award publications

In a few days' time it would be Debbie's birthday. Her mother had promised that this year she could have a party in the garden, so Debbie was very busy sending out invitations to all her friends. Here's what she wrote in them:

"Please come to Debbie's party next Wednesday at 3 o'clock. There'll be music, games, and lots of surprises!"

Her brother Daniel and best friend Lisa helped her to seal the envelopes and stick on the stamps.

"This one's nearly the last," said Debbie. "What a lot there are—my wrist's beginning to ache. But I don't think I've forgotten anyone."

All Debbie's friends said that they would love to come, and as her birthday drew nearer she began to get things ready for the party.

"Come and try on your new dress," her mother said.

"Look out—it's full of pins, so don't fidget."

Debbie thought the pink dress looked lovely—she had chosen the material herself.

Daniel and Peter, his next-door neighbor, started to put up a stall in the garden. They found some old striped curtains for the awning, so that it looked like a sideshow at a fair, and planned to see how many cans Debbie's friends could knock down with one throw.

The day before her birthday Debbie went to the hairdresser. It was the first time she had had a shampoo and set, and she felt very grown up as she sat under the drier. She tried to read a book, but her thoughts were racing. . . How was Mother getting on with the food? Would there be enough for everyone? Had she iced the cake yet? Debbie was beginning to feel very excited.

As soon as her hair was dry Debbie raced home. There was still plenty for her to do in the kitchen. Daniel watched as she piped whipped cream onto the trifles and jellies. He hoped there might be some left over for him!

At last the day came! If something had been forgotten, it was too late to do anything about it now.

The door bell rang. "Happy birthday Debbie," said Ben.

It rang again... and again. "Happy birthday," said Kathy, and Tom, and all the others.

Debbie could hardly hold all her gaily wrapped presents.

Debbie thanked her friends over and over again.
She was so happy to see them all.
Once more the door bell rang. It was the man from the flower shop. He handed her a bunch of beautiful roses—they matched Debbie's dress perfectly. She found a card inside. It said, "Have a lovely party, Debbie. We'll be thinking of you.
With love from Grandma and Grandpa."

It was time for the games to start in the garden. First was blindman's-bluff. Debbie was blind-folded. Then feeling about in all directions, she tried to catch someone. "Look out!" She tripped over Ben. "Got you," she said. "It's your turn now."

Now they were fishing for bottles with a curtain ring tied to the end of a fishing rod. It was Tom's turn now. He had almost done it, but it wasn't easy trying to slide the ring over the bottle.

Debbie had been teaching her dog Timmy some tricks to entertain her friends. They watched in delight as he stood on his hind legs, balancing a ball on the tip of his nose. What an amazing dog—they could hardly believe their eyes! "Sideshows first, and now a circus! Whatever will happen next?" asked Kathy, full of excitement.

"Time to eat," said Debbie. She'd put on a white apron and was handing out the drinks while Daniel had dressed up as a chef to carry in a plate of cakes. "Try one of those—they're really delicious. I made them myself," he said to Jane.

Nothing had been forgotten to make the party a great success. "Come on there's a hat here for everyone!" Debbie called as she put a paper hat on Sarah's head. "Just help yourselves." But she could hardly hear herself speak. Tom, wearing a duck mask, was blowing a trumpet right into her ear.

Debbie's parents had given her a record player for her birthday—just what she had wanted. "Let's have some music," said Debbie, looking through her records. "This one should be good. Make a big circle, and then we can all dance."

Timmy, in the middle of the ring, had got caught up in some paper streamers. As the children danced round him, he became more and more tangled. They roared with laughter at his antics as he struggled to get free. He was enjoying playing the clown. "What fun this is," Lisa said. And they all agreed.

As it began to get dark Debbie's mother lit the candles on the birthday cake. There were eight of them. Everyone sang "Happy birthday to you," and clapped when Debbie took only one breath to blow them all out. In no time at all every slice of cake had disappeared—it was delicious. But the final surprise was yet to come. . .

Not even Debbie knew about this surprise. Daddy had been secretly preparing a firework show to make a dazzling finish to a lovely party. There were rockets, and roman candles, and catherine wheels. . . the children's eyes gleamed as the fireworks whizzed and crackled above their heads, lighting up the sky with red, white and blue flashes.

It was a wonderful end to a marvellous day. Tired but happy,
Debbie thought about everything that had happened. Surely it
had been the best birthday party in the world. And she had a
whole year to remember it.